Bad Boris
and the birthday

A Beaver Book

Published by Arrow Books Limited
62-65 Chandos Place, London WC2N 4NW

An imprint of Century Hutchinson Ltd

London Melbourne Sydney Auckland
Johannesburg and agencies throughout the world

First published by Hutchinson Children's Books 1987

Beaver edition 1989

© Susie Jenkin-Pearce 1987

Printed and bound in Great Britain
by Scotprint, Musselburgh, Scotland

ISBN 0 09 957200 1

Bad Boris
and the birthday

Susie Jenkin-Pearce

Beaver Books

To Caroline

One morning, Boris looked at the calendar. 'Do you know what?' he said. 'I think it's somebody's birthday today.'
  'Whose?' asked the kitten.
  'It must be Maisie's,' said Boris. 'Let's bake her a cake.'

'What goes into cakes?' said the kitten.

'Sugar,' said Boris. 'Lots and Lots.'

'And eggs?' asked the kitten.

'Yes,' said Boris. 'And flour and milk and jam and currants and butter and cherries and raisins.'

'Yum!' said the kitten.

Soon there was nothing left in the larder.

So Boris and the kitten set off for the shop.

Boris knew exactly what to buy, he tried to be careful but...

'Watch out!' cried an angry shopper.

'Baking a cake?' asked the lady at the till.
  'Yes!' said Boris proudly. 'It's for Maisie's birthday.
It's a surprise!'

It was hard carrying everything in the small basket.

'There's not much left,' said the kitten.
   'Oh there's plenty,' said Boris. 'Just watch me.'
   He threw all the ingredients into a bowl and began to mix.

'Right, it's lovely and slurpy,' said Boris when he had finished. 'Into the oven.'

'It's done…I think,'
said the kitten.

'What colour icing shall we have?'
'Green is nice,' said Boris.

Just then Maisie came home.
   'Boris!' she gasped. 'What an awful mess!
Whatever have you been doing?'

'We were only trying to make you a birthday cake,' he said,
bursting into tears. 'It was supposed to be a surprise.'
    Maisie began to smile.

'But it's *your* birthday today Boris, not mine,' she said.

'Oh Maisie, weren't we silly?' said Boris. 'Fancy an elephant forgetting his own birthday. But I won't forget again, and just wait until it *is* your birthday. Now that we've had some practice we can make the best birthday cake ever!'

And with one puff from Boris, the candle flames were gone.

Boris's Birthday Cake Recipe

1. Lots of flour

2. Lots of water

3. Bake until black

4. Ask Maisie!

Maisie's Birthday Cake Recipe

¾ lb butter
½ lb sugar
4 eggs
¾ lb flour
½ teaspoon mixed spice
Pinch of salt
¼ lb raisins

¼ lb cherries
¼ lb sultanas
¼ lb peel
¼ lb chopped almonds
Grated rind of ½ a lemon
Grated rind of ½ an orange
3–4 tablespoons of milk

Size of tin, 8" by 3"

Method

Beat the butter and sugar to a cream; add each egg separately and beat until the mixture is stiff and uniform. Sift together flour, mixed spice and salt, stir well into creamed mixture. Add raisins, cherries cut into halves, sultanas, and the peel and almonds chopped into small pieces, also the orange and lemon rind and the milk. Mix the ingredients thoroughly and bake in a tin, well lined with greased paper, for 3½ hours at gas mark 2 (150°C/300°F).

Icing

Mix icing sugar (about 4 oz) with tepid water, to form a coating consistency. Add colouring, and spread icing on the cake with a knife dipped in hot water.

Other titles in the Beaver/Sparrow Picture Book series: